Robert White

The Battle of Flodden, fought 9. Sept. 1513

Anatiposi

Robert White

The Battle of Flodden, fought 9. Sept. 1513

Reprint of the original.

1st Edition 2023 | ISBN: 978-3-38230-324-2

Anatiposi Verlag is an imprint of Outlook Verlagsgesellschaft mbH.

Verlag (Publisher): Outlook Verlag GmbH, Zeilweg 44, 60439 Frankfurt, Deutschland
Vertretungsberechtigt (Authorized to represent): E. Roepke, Zeilweg 44, 60439 Frankfurt, Deutschland
Druck (Print): Books on Demand GmbH, In de Tarpen 42, 22848 Norderstedt, Deutschland

THE

Battle of Flodden,

FOUGHT 9 SEPT. 1513.

BY ROBERT WHITE.

From the "Archæologia Æliana," Vol. iii., New Ser

NEWCASTLE-UPON-TYNE:
PRINTED BY THOMAS PIGG AND CO., CLAYTON STREET.

1859.

To Moneylaws

To Coldstream

To Thorntington

To Coldstream

Kings Stone

Pallinsburn House

Hills

Pit of Bones X

BATTLE FIELD

Branxton Hill

Vicarage

Branxton Monument

To Milfield

N O R

Cannon Ball found here

BRANXTON

P A L E

Wild Road

Pond

Marden

Windy Law

Kings Chair Hill

Kings Castle

To ford

F L O D D E N

H I L L

F O R K

Crookham

Blue Bell

To Wooler

MAP OF
FLODDEN FIELD
No 1 To Accompany
Rev. R. Jones

The Battle of Flodden.

FOUGHT 9 SEPTEMBER, 1513

During the reign of James IV., which extended from 1488 to 1513, Scotland underwent great improvement in the arts and in the general administration of justice. The entrance of that monarch into public life was unfavourable; for, about his seventeenth year, he appeared in arms against his father, when the latter was slain, and by way of atonement for such error, he occasionally shut himself up for days in religious seclusion, and wore around his body an iron chain, to which he annexed some additional weight every year. But when such periods of penance were over, he entered freely into society, and by his bland deportment to the nobles, and kindly bearing to the lowest of his subjects, he was much beloved and highly honoured. His love of sports and frolicksome disposition gained him, wherever he went, the cordial sympathy and attachment of his people. He paid much attention to the art of healing, and prided himself upon being the best curer of wounds in his dominions. By his great constitutional vigour and temperate living, he practised with success all bodily exercises; and such was the order he maintained in his kingdom, that, with his cloak thrown around him and his hunting-knife by his side, he could have mounted on horseback, and, without a single attendant, travelled upwards of a hundred miles in perfect safety. Though no great scholar himself, he well knew the value of learning; for having a natural son, instead of appointing him to any office of civil importance, he placed him at Padua, in Italy, under charge of the celebrated Erasmus, and such were the acquirements of the youth, that by the influence of his father and the authority of Pope Julius II., he was appointed, at an early age, Archbishop of St. Andrew's. At this period, in Scotland, considerable encouragement was given to literature; for the University of Aberdeen was now founded, and the king granted pensions, besides other gifts, to Blind Harry, the metrical historian of Wallace, and to William Dunbar, a poet who in graphic ability and Horatian terseness of expression has not yet been surpassed, even by Robert Burns. But no better proof can be adduced of the progress of letters in Scotland during this reign, than that Gawin Douglas completed in Scottish verse his translation of Virgil's *Æneid* about two months prior to the fatal battle of Flodden.

All this time England was making equally great progress in art and science; though up to the close of the fifteenth century, with exception of Chaucer, she had no popular versifyers or bards able to compete with Barbour and Dunbar. Some slight differences existed between Henry VII. and James the Scottish king, his son-in-law; but the former by his prudence soothed the haughty spirit of the latter, without allowing trifles to appear of importance. Not so, however, with his imperious successor, Henry VIII., whose presumption and power readily afforded matter of complaint to James, but unfortunately the latter was unsuccessful in obtaining redress. For example, John, commonly called the Bastard Heron, having been implicated during the preceding reign in the murder of Sir Robert Ker, a Scottish warden, and especial favourite of the king, for whose crime his brother, Sir William Heron of Ford, remained a prisoner in Scotland, was allowed to go at large in England, and lead bands of outlaws across the Border for the sole object of plunder. Again, the Bartons, a seafaring family, whose father's vessel, in 1479, had been seized by a squadron belonging to Portugal, obtained letters of reprisal, and captured ships from that kingdom; but complaints having been made at the court of England that her commerce was thereby obstructed, a couple of war-ships were selected to repress the grievance. They were commanded by Lord Thomas Howard and Sir Edward Howard, sons of the Earl of Surrey, and these captains falling in with Andrew Barton in the Downs, who was returning with one ship and an armed pinnace from a cruise on the coast of Portugal, gave him battle, and after a desperate conflict, in which Barton was killed, his craft and guns were taken, and employed in the navy of England. This was considered a great insult to James, who felt proud of his maritime influence, and when he demanded immediate satisfaction, an evasive reply from Henry was all he could obtain. The circumstance tended probably to irritate him the more, from the contrast it presented to his own conduct on a similar occasion. In 1491 Henry VII., annoyed at the success of the Scottish flag, and the bravery of Sir Andrew Wood, gave command of three large ships to Stephen Bull, who undertook to bring this Scottish rover of the seas to England dead or alive. Bull took his position behind an island in the Forth, ardently awaiting for his prey. Wood, with two vessels, hove in sight, and a most determined battle took place, which continued for two days, and the vessels drifting northward to the mouth of the Tay, the three ships of England, with their crews, were captured, and carried into Dundee. The victor handed over Bull and his prizes to the Scottish monarch, who gave the adventurous captain and his people gifts, and sent him with the ships as a present to the King of England.

But beyond such differences as these, the main cause of dissension between the two kingdoms was the adherence of Scotland to the interest of France. About the beginning of 1513, Henry VIII. having entered into a confederacy with others who interfered in the quarrel between Pope Julius and Louis XII. of France, it was evident he meditated an invasion of that kingdom, and the King of Scotland employed every means to ward off the danger which threatened his old ally. He even proposed to his haughty brother-in-law a remission of all offences and damages suffered by his people, and afterwards observed that Henry might command every ship in his possession if he would abandon his hostile design upon France. Although rejecting these terms, Henry was desirous that James should remain quiet, and appointed Thomas Lord Dacre of Gilsland, and Dr. West, to conciliate and endeavour, if possible, to remove the differences which existed between the two countries. The latter proceeded to Scotland for that purpose, and when there exerted his influence to withdraw King James from the alliance with France. On this point, however, the latter continued immoveable, and after repeated attempts at negociation, West at last departed from Scotland, bearing with him letters from the king and queen. Henry was earnestly entreated thereby to make peace with Louis, or at least to defer his expedition to France for one year, and the queen in a spirited epistle upbraided her brother for his meanness in withholding a legacy of valuable jewels left to her by her father. The English monarch in reply accused James warmly on the rupture he had made of perpetual peace, to which both kings had previously sworn, yet he was inclined to pacific measures if they were practicable. In the meantime, having on the 6th and 16th of June sent off two divisions of troops to France, he set sail with the third on the 30th of that month, and soon after was stationed on his enemy's country at the head of an army of twenty-five thousand fighting men.

James all along suspecting the wilful disposition of the English king, was steadily preparing for war. He determined in the first place to assist France; and having bestowed great attention in the equipment of his navy, when tidings reached him of Henry's departure, he ordered his fleet, amounting to nearly twenty vessels, to prepare for sea, and be placed at the service of that kingdom. It sailed on the 24th of July with three thousand troops on board, under command of the Earl of Arran. Those ships—the only fleet which Scotland ever prepared for war—by the perverse guidance of the commander, did not reach France till after the battle of Flodden was fought. On the same day when the vessels sailed, James addressed another letter to Henry, who was now preparing to besiege Terouenne, complaining of injuries and grievances, and in an urgent tone desiring him to return to his own dominions, else, on behalf of France, he should be compelled to desist from his purpose. The missive reached its destination in due time, and the King of England replied with considerable warmth, but the answer did not arrive in Scotland till after the death of the king.

Here it may be necessary to examine the position of James, and ascertain the causes why he adhered so closely to France. That kingdom had the policy to maintain a friendly intimacy with Scotland, sending her often provisions and arms, and assisting her in various ways as occasion required. Such acts of kindness, at a time when commercial intercourse was yet in its infancy, almost effaced the remembrance of the injury Scotland sustained on account of the former country at Neville's Cross, upwards of one hundred and sixty years before, and whatever might occur, James considered France a sure stay in case of adversity. He was likewise sagacious enough to perceive that if the arms of England were successful in overturning the state of that kingdom, Scotland might anticipate slight amity from a conqueror who was not likely to respect any barrier which stood in the way of his power or ambition. Besides all this, the king possessed great bravery, with a high sense of honour, and being slow to perceive any evil in those upon whom he bestowed confidence, the frank openness of his character tended to make him the dupe of crafty and designing men. In this way Andrew Forman, Bishop of Moray, won over by the gold and promises of France, brought all his influence to bear upon the king's weakness, and unhappily was too successful. This prelate had been sent to almost every court in Europe connected with Scotland, and by the most authentic of our historians, he is believed not only to have urged the king to his ruin, but to have sacrificed the interest of his country to his own worldly aggrandizement. He had been despatched as ambassador to France, and his aims were seconded by another favourite of the king, De la Motte, a French statesman, and a warrior both by sea and land. The latter was in the habit of bringing vessels laden with provisions to Scotland, and besides he captured by sea many English prizes, which he likewise conveyed thither.

It thus fell out that when the English armies landed on the soil of

France, that country redoubled her efforts to enlist Scotland in her cause. De la Motte accordingly arrived in Scotland with ships laden with wine and corn for the benefit of her people, but the most valuable portion of his freight consisted of a large quantity of crowns of the sun, a French golden coinage, which he distributed liberally to King James and his court. By way also of playing upon the temper of the king, with infinite skill, La Motte brought him a letter from the Queen of France, in which she represented herself as a high-born damsel in distress to her own true knight, saying she had suffered much in defence of his honour, and requested him for her sake to march with his army three feet upon English ground. This letter was accompanied by a precious ring from her own finger, valued at fifteen thousand French crowns. At the same time Bishop Forman, by letter also, remonstrated with his sovereign that his honour was for ever lost unless he assisted France, as he, the said dignitary, had promised in his name.

With exception of those who had been recipients of, and were influenced by the gold of France, the council of James, formed of his principal nobility, were opposed to a declaration of war against England, but the king would not listen to any pacific measure. He therefore summoned the whole military array of his kingdom to meet him within three weeks at the Borough Moor, near Edinburgh, with provisions for forty days. Scotland at that time, through the whole length and breadth of her boundaries, must have presented an animating spectacle. A thousand anvils rang from morning to night preparing armour and weapons; swords, spears, and axes were sharpened in every village; and many noble dames in hall and bower were busily employed, embroidering flags and pennons under which their lords were about to advance into England. It is said, when the multitude assembled they amounted to a hundred thousand men—a great army to raise from so small a kingdom, but all the attendants and camp followers were undoubtedly included in that number. Tidings of these warlike preparations being circulated in England, a marauding party from Northumberland crossed over into Scotland, and, as a commencement to hostilities, brought off considerable spoil. Upon this, Alexander Lord Home, Warden of the Marches, and Chamberlain of Scotland, having called together nearly three thousand men upon horseback, entered England by way of retaliation, and burned seven villages, besides collecting much plunder. Some detachments from the main body of the marauders hastened home with what they had secured, but as Lord Home and his immediate adherents were returning in a careless manner through the level plain of Millfield, they were attacked near Broomhouse by a large party of horse-archers and others under command of Sir William Bulmer, the High Sheriff of the Bishoprick, who had been sent by the Earl of Surrey to defend the frontier. Cunningly concealing themselves among the long broom through which the path lay, they assailed the bands of straggling Scots, who were encumbered with booty, and killing nearly four hundred, took about two hundred prisoners, and put the remainder to flight. Home fled, but lost his banner, while his brother George was among the captives, and all the prey, comprising a large number of horses, was recovered by the English. This encounter took place on the 13th of August, and in Scotland the movement was generally known as "The Ill Rode."

Such a misfortune, with other singular, but very remarkable occurrences, tended to cloud the mind of the king, who was open to superstition, but did not prevent him from following out his martial design. As he sat engaged in his devotions in the church of Linlithgo, which adjoins the palace, a venerable personage, advanced in years, and wearing a primitive dress, came before him, and with an air of divine authority, warned him of the danger of invading England. A supernatural summons, also, at midnight, echoed from the cross of Edinburgh, calling by name the chief men of Scotland, who subsequently fell at Flodden field. The queen likewise dreamed she had seen the king fall from a great precipice, and that she lost one of her eyes; but all these premonitions, united to her entreaties that he would not enter into hostile collision with her brother, failed of effect. Animated by high chivalric daring, he considered the contempt shown to him by England deserved to be checked. It is true, that he and his people for the course of a generation were unaccustomed to war; but on reviewing his gallant army upon the Borough Moor, the sight thereof might well flatter the pride of a king. The known bravery and undoubted loyalty of chief and vassal, should he march to the south, afforded him a fair prospect of success.

Neither before nor since did ever Scotland furnish an army of fighting men like those who were collected at that time on the Borough Moor. Owing to the authority exercised by the sheriffs and bailiffs of the several counties, in observing that the troops were properly arrayed for war, they presented a most formidable appearance. The principal leaders and men at arms were mounted on able horses; the Border prickers rode those of a less size, but remarkably active. These wore mail, chiefly of plate, from head to heel; that of the higher ranks being wrought and polished with great elegance, while the Borderers had armour of a very light description. All the others were on foot, and the

burgesses of the towns wore what was called white armour, consisting of
steel cap, gorget and mail brightly burnished, fitting gracefully to the
body, and covering the limbs and hands. The yeomen or peasantry
had the sallat or iron cap, the hauberk or plate jack, formed of thin
flat pieces of iron quilted below leather or linen, which covered the
legs and arms, and they had gloves likewise. The Highlanders
were not so well defended by armour, though the chiefs were partly
armed like their southern brethren, retaining, however, the eagle's
feather in the bonnet, and wearing, like their followers, the tartan and
the belted plaid. Almost every soldier had a large shield or target for
defence, and wore the white cross of Saint Andrew, either on his breast
or some other prominent place. The offensive arms were the spear five
yards in length, the long pike, the mace or mallet, two-handed and
other swords, the dagger, the knife, the bow and sheaf of arrows; while
the Danish axe, with a broad flat spike on the opposite side to the edge,
was peculiar to the Islesmen, and the studded targe to the Highlanders.

King James at length putting his train of artillery into motion, which
consisted of twenty-two pieces, chiefly drawn by oxen, marched to the
south as light-hearted as he had been about to take part in a tournament,
and crossing the Tweed near Coldstream, he entered upon his enemy's
ground on Monday the 22nd day of August. The next two days, unless
he employed a part of the time in besieging Wark Castle, would appear
to have been inactively spent; for on Wednesday the 24th, he was at
Twysel-haugh, and there issued an edict that the heirs of all who fell in
that expedition should have "ward, relief and marriage of the king free."
Thence leading his forces down the Tweed, he laid siege to Norham Castle,
and speedily gaining the outworks, demolished one of its towers, killed
several of its defenders, and the fortress surrendered to him on Monday
the 29th. Remaining there probably till the next day, to secure the
plunder, for a large quantity was stowed up in the place, he moved
westward, and captured Wark Castle, bordering upon the Tweed, about
two miles above Cornhill. Then the king led his army against the
castle of Etal, which also surrendered, and if we suppose that three
days were thus spent in obtaining possession of the last two strongholds,
on Friday the 2nd, or at latest on Saturday the 3rd of September, suit
was made to him by Elizabeth Heron, wife of Sir William Heron, that
the house or castle of Ford, where she resided, might not be assaulted
or thrown down. It would appear he agreed to the proposition, that if
at any time before noon on Monday the 5th of September, she, the said
Elizabeth, would cause to be delivered up to him the Lord Johnstone
and Alexander Hume, then prisoners in England, the castle should

stand without being burned or spoiled. Occupied as the king was in conducting his army within an enemy's boundaries, it is unlikely that any correspondence between him and Lady Heron would be opened up until he was beleaguering Etal Castle, and the week then must have been far advanced.[1] If they met, it would appear to have been for a short period, for the lady departed to meet the Earl of Surrey, who assented to the conditions at Alnwick on Sunday the 4th of September.

Two weeks were thus spent in assaulting, taking, plundering, and throwing down two or three Border castles, without effecting any other important movement. Never before had such a force of armed men who belonged Scotland crossed the Tweed, and never before did any Scottish army, however small in numbers, inflict for the time so little injury upon England. Had the king been actuated by something of the spirit of Bruce, or that of the great leaders under that noble warrior, he might have penetrated to York, and, besides plundering Newcastle and Durham, swept the country and returned unharmed again to his own kingdom. The weather, be it remembered, was exceedingly unfavourable, for great cold and wind prevailed, and rain poured down almost every hour from the time of entering England; but this had not prevented James from carrying out any extended warlike measure, and it is apparent that though he drew the sword, he did not aim at striking a decisive blow. Undoubtedly he expected no opposition from England, and to march in a hostile manner upon her soil, to demolish some of her fortresses, to make known where he went his prowess and chivalric bearing, and to exhibit the pomp and splendour of his army south of the Tweed, seems to have been the extent of his ambition, for during the period of his absence from his own land, he never penetrated more than seven or eight miles beyond the line which separates the two kingdoms.

When Henry VIII. sailed to France he appointed Thomas Earl of Surrey, Lieutenant-general of the Northern Counties, telling him not to be negligent, and to place no dependance upon the Scots. Such a charge could not possibly have devolved upon one better qualified to perform it. He was an old man in his sixty-ninth year, and acquainted with war, having, with his father the Duke of Norfolk, commanded the

---

[1] The evidence supplied both by Lindsay of Pitscottie, and Buchanan, on the king's improper intimacy with Lady Heron, is certainly strong; but the time noted in the text is given according to our chronicles, and the reader may consult notes on this subject both in Lingard's *History* and in the *Pictorial History of England*, also an excellent little volume, Oliver's (Chatto's) *Rambles in Northumberland*. If report spake true, James acted ungallantly to throw down the lady's castle, after stipulating to preserve it.

archers in the army of Richard III. at Bosworth field, on which occasion
his said father was slain. The threatening attitude of Scotland was
well known in England, and Surrey collecting his adherents and tenants
together, numbering five hundred men, rode through London with them
on the 22nd day of July, and came to the castle of Pontefract, west of
York, on the 1st of August. Without delay he ordered Sir William
Bulmer, already mentioned, to proceed to the Borders with two hundred
archers on horseback, and remain there in the strongholds ready to
meet the foe. Thomas Lord Dacre, who had spies in his service, was
also placed to give intimation of any advance of the enemy. Calling,
therefore, the wisest and most intelligent noblemen and gentlemen
left in the kingdom to his assistance, Surrey, by their advice and
approval, made every preparation for defence, arranging with Sir Philip
Tylney, who was his brother-in-law, how the troops should be paid, and
directing Sir Nicholas Appleyard, Master of the Ordnance, how the artillery should be dispatched to the North. He also commanded all
lords spiritual and temporal, with knights and others who had tenants
or the command of towns, to enumerate the men under each who could
be horsed and harnessed at an hour's notice, and ordered them to attend
upon himself. Moreover, he appointed posts everywhere over the
northern parts, that he might have that portion of the kingdom under
his immediate controul. Equally great was the commotion over England with what has been told of Scotland. Every province of the North
resounded with tidings of war, the people were in excellent heart on
the stirring occasion, old and young men got ready their armour, females
lent their assistance, and Queen Catherine herself, in a letter to Wolsey,
dated the 13th of August, stated, "she was horrible busy with making
standards, banners, and badges."

It has been said that King James crossed the Tweed on the 22nd day
of August, tidings of which reached the Earl of Surrey early on Thursday the 25th, with the addition that his army were wasting the English
Borders. On the same day Surrey wrote to all the northern gentlemen
to be with him at Newcastle, with their followers, on Thursday the 1st
day of September, and with his retinue of five hundred men he proceeded onward from Pontefract to York. On the following day he advanced to the North, amid such foul weather that his guide was almost
drowned. During his stay at Durham he learned with much sorrow
that Norham Castle had yielded to the Scots, and on the succeeding
night the wind blew so furiously, he was afraid his eldest son, Lord
Thomas Howard, Admiral of England, who had promised to meet him
at Newcastle with a large number of men, would be lost at sea. But

on the 30th day of August he heard mass, and by consent of the prior, obtained, for the ensuing struggle, Saint Cuthbert's banner, which was borne by Sir John Forster—that ancient hallowed relic which before had waved over several battle fields, and was considered a sure pledge of victory. That day, being Tuesday, he moved forward to Newcastle, where he met Lord Dacre, Sir William Bulmer, Sir Marmaduke Constable, and others, upon whom he relied as councillors, and resolved that on Sunday the 4th of September he should take the field at Bolton, in Northumberland, a few miles west of Alnwick. The counties of Cheshire, Yorkshire, Lancashire, Westmorland, Cumberland, and other places throughout England, now contributed their forces of armed men, who came forward in vast numbers.[2] Boys even did what they could in the great cause of defence, for Henry Jenkins, about his eleventh year, who lived to be the oldest man upon record in England, was sent from the southern part of Richmondshire to Northallerton with a horse-load of arrows. Troops were crossing the Tyne hourly, and as Newcastle had slender accommodation for large numbers of men, the Earl of Surrey quitted that town to make room for those who were entering it, and journeying onward, he reached Alnwick on Saturday the 3rd of September. Inclement weather prevented the forces arriving in due time; hence he lingered during the next day in that town, when his son, the Lord Admiral, joined him with a large number of brave captains, hardy mariners, and others, wearing black armour, with St. George's cross floating above them. This reinforcement was most acceptable to the earl, who, calling his council together, proceeded to determine the order in which he should meet the enemy. Here, by cordial and general approval, he wrote to the King of Scotland, assenting to the proposition made by Elizabeth Heron to deliver up the Lord Johnstone and Alexander Hume, on condition that Ford Castle should neither be spoiled nor demolished. He further agreed that if King James would give up to Elizabeth Heron her husband, who was then a prisoner, as already stated, he the earl would cause to be delivered in exchange Sir George Hume and William Carr. The earl also observed, that as the King of Scotland had invaded his brother's realm, casting down castles and murdering his subjects, battle would be offered him on Friday first, as he, Surrey, was true knight to God and the king. With this missive, Thomas the Lord Admiral empowered Rouge Croix, a pursuivant-at-

<hr>

[2] It would appear that there were men from all parts of England in the army. John Winchcombe, the famous clothier of Newbury, in Berkshire, commonly called "Jack of Newbury" was present, accompanied by a hundred of his own men, all armed and clothed at his expence. The kindling spirit of English patriotism extended much farther than the northern counties.

arms, wearing the red cross of St. George, to shew King James, that as he had been blamed on days of truce in not making redress for vanquishing Andrew Barton, he was now come personally to justify the death of that pirate, and would be found in the front of the battle, where he would give no quarter, save to the king's own person. It may be observed that a trumpeter accompanied the messenger when he was dispatched to the Scottish camp.

Accordingly, on Monday the 5th of September, the Earl of Surrey took his field at Bolton, where all the noblemen and others met him with their retinues, amounting to upwards of twenty-six thousand men. King James detained the English pursuivant, and sent Islay, his own herald, who was not allowed to approach Bolton, but on arrival of the trumpeter, Surrey despatched York herald with him to Mile, westward, at a distance from the camp. On the morning of Tuesday, Surrey, accompanied by the leaders of the army, each having a servant man to hold his horse, went thither, and gave Islay audience. The Scottish herald showed that King James gave no answer to the application for preserving Ford Castle, but he the earl was welcome as any nobleman in England respecting battle, and that if the king had received his letter at Edinburgh, he would have come and fulfilled the earl's desire upon the appointed day. To the forward message of the Lord Admiral, he the king did not condescend to make any reply. Islay then delivered a brief note written by the king's secretary, relating that his brother the King of England had broken peace first with him—that in vain he had required him to amend, and warning him of his conduct, he took this for his quarrel, which by the grace of God he should defend. The Earl of Surrey, on learning that James accepted his offer of battle, was right joyous, and praising the courage of the king, offered to be bound in a large sum of money he would not fail of his intention.[3] After some arrangement about

[3] Surrey seemed desirous above all things to bring the Scots to battle. In addition to his proposal that he and good surety with him should be bound in ten thousand pounds sterling towards the accomplishment thereof, the earl also observed that failing his promise, the following disgrace might be put upon him, and as it illustrates the early meaning of the word "baffle," the quotation is supplied from Hall:—"And farthermore the Earle bad the Heraulde for to saye to his maister, that yf he for his parte kept not hys appoyntmente, then he was content that the Scottes shoulde Baffull hym, which is a great reproche amonge the Scottes, and is used when a man is openly perjured, and then they make of hym an image paynted reuersed, with hys heles upwarde, wyth hys name, wonderynge, cryenge, and blowing out of hym with hornes, in the most dispitefull maner they can. In token that he is worthy to be exiled the compaignie of all good creatures." Fol. xl.

Shakspeare had undoubtedly the above passage in remembrance when he penned the following:—

"PRINCE. Where shall we take a purse to-morrow, Jack?

"FALSTAFF. Where thou wilt, lad, I'll make one; an I do not, call me villain and baffle me." *Henry IV*. Part Second. Act I. Scene II.

the safe return of the herald, the earl returned to the camp, and sent the whole army forward in suitable order of battle to Wooler-haugh, where they lodged that night.

We may here avail ourselves of a passing glance at the armed men who three days afterwards vanquished the power of Scotland near Branxton. The Earl of Surrey, as he is shown on the evening before the battle, in the *Memorials, &c of the Howard Family*, has his helmet placed before him with feathers flowing down behind, a sort of *tippet-like* plate covering the shoulders, whereon the white lion is conspicuous, other plates round his body descending nearly to the knee, showing also his blazonings, and leg armour to the toes, the plates of which at that place are very broad, and at the heels are large pointed spurs. Again, the nobility, knights, and men at arms were on horseback, each accompanied by attendants according to his rank. They wore also plate armour from head to foot, some sorts of which, belonging to superior men, were brightly polished and occasionally inlaid with silver or gold, while their steeds were richly caparisoned with housings embroidered with the devices of their respective owners. Among the spearmen and billmen, who were on foot, plate mail had given way to armour, similar to that mentioned previously as prevailing in the Scottish army, being composed of small steel or iron plates, of a square form, overlapping each other, and quilted either upon or within linen or leather. Such a covering was flexible, yielding to every turn of the body, and kept the wearer often safe from the thrust of a spear or the stroke of a sword. Many of the archers wore the brigantine or jack, like the spearmen or billmen, while others, as in the preceding reign, were "clad in a shirt of chain mail with very wide sleeves, and over this a small vest of red cloth laced in front, with hose on the leg and braces on the left arm." The horsemen had the mace or battle axe in addition to the lance, the sword, and dagger. The spearman, whose name indicates the weapon he bore, had also the sword and dagger, and indeed the two latter were girded on almost every soldier in the army. The two-handed sword was not in much request; but of the several arms mentioned, the most effective was the large bill—a strong blade with an edge from eighteen to twenty-four inches long, mounted on a handle of sufficient length, and wielded by the powerful and able-bodied peasantry of England. The archer, again, with his bow cased in coarse cloth, and a sheaf of arrows, beside the dagger and sword, on the hilt of which was usually a small buckler, had often a leaden mell which he bore at his back, and as the bow was useless in close combat, such a hammer was often fatal as the great bill. According to the fashion of the previous reign, white was the prevailing hue of the whole army, save that of the mariners brought by the admiral, and all wore the red cross of St. George, except a dignitary of the church or an officer at arms.

King James, in the meantime, after the castles of Norham, Wark, and Etal had been taken and spoiled, came with his army before that of Ford, and whether it was through revenge of the death of Sir Robert Ker, or that the Lord Johnstone and Alexander Hume were not delivered up to him by noon on the 5th of September, or that the English army were at hand, it would be difficult to know, but he threw down the stronghold, by the falling of the timbers whereof, several of his men were injured. About this time large numbers of the army, having ravaged the adjoining country, whence they collected much booty and took many prisoners, owing to the continued severity of the weather, forsook their colours, and covertly retired with their spoil into Scotland. Those who remained, consisting chiefly of the superior men of the kingdom, and their immediate tenants or followers, were encamped on the grounds below Ford, and on the king receiving the hostile message from Surrey, a council was held to decide what measures ought to be adopted. The most sagacious of the nobles, among whom were Lord Patrick Lindsay, and Archibald Sixth Earl of Angus, called "Bell the Cat," concurred in the opinion that the army should return home instantly with what booty they had acquired. The main reason for this was, that the numbers of the army were now greatly reduced, and intelligence had reached them of the superiority in this respect of the enemy. Lindsay alluded to the imprudence of bringing all the nobility and gentry of Scotland into battle against Surrey and so many common English people, showing the danger to which his own country would be liable in case of defeat, and the slight honour which would accrue to her were they victorious. He advocated this point most forcibly in an apologue of a merchant playing at hazard with a gambler, wherein he likened their monarch to a rose-noble and Surrey to a bent halfpenny, being, as he said, "an old crooked carle sitting in a chariot," which might not be far from the truth. Angus, a veteran of sage experience, observed the king had already gained great honour; that the object for which they came into England had been fully accomplished; that great benefit had been rendered to their ally by drawing off and retaining for this occasion such a large English army; that if they returned home they would be better able to cope with the enemy in their own land; and besides, in their present strength, they would keep the English constantly on the watch, and no higher service than this could possibly be rendered to France. Hereupon the king was very angry, for

he threatened Lindsay with death on returning to Scotland, maintaining he would fight the English if they were one hundred thousand
strong, and telling Angus if he was afraid he might go home—a taunt
which the old warrior felt keenly, for it is said he burst into tears; but
availing himself of the liberty granted, he retired, leaving behind him
his two eldest sons, and a large body of his name and kindred, as pledges
of loyalty to his sovereign. Looking, however, at the matter, in its
various bearings, and taking into consideration the probable inferiority
of his strength in point of numbers to the English, King James forth-
with removed his camp to Flodden hill, a commanding position about
two miles south-west of the former place. A battery of guns was
planted on the east, to defend the bridge over the Till at Ford, and a
square line of defence was thrown up round the camp, the traces of
which are still visible. Here, on the evening of the 8th of September,
he was joined by the Earl of Caithness, who brought with him three
hundred young warriors all dressed in green.[4]

In the *Memorials, &c. of the Howard Family* already alluded to, the Earl
of Surrey is represented, on the morning before the Battle of Flodden,
kneeling upon a cushion in the attitude of prayer; but one may suppose
that when engaged in strife a steady but vengeful fire would glow from
his dark eyes, as if it would scorch up his enemies. Had he been desirous
to spare the effusion of blood, it had been well on his part could he
have induced the King of Scotland to depart peaceably to his own land.
But this he was eager to prevent, as if conscious that his own army
were superior to that of Scotland, and above every other consideration,
he seemed wishful that James should remain. So intently he appears to
have sought mortal combat, that it may almost be suspected some serious
affront had been put upon him by the king, which could only be expi-
ated by blood, but of this there is no trace on the side of James, who
uniformly treated the earl with courtesy and kindness. Ten years be-

---

[4] This incident is related in a note appended to Dr. Leyden's beautiful *Ode on
Visiting Flodden :—*

"Under the vigorous administration of James IV., the young Earl of Caithness
incurred the penalty of outlawry and forfeiture, for revenging an ancient feud. On
the evening preceding the battle of Flodden, accompanied by three hundred young
warriors, arrayed in green, he presented himself before the king, and submitted to his
mercy. This mark of attachment was so agreeable to that warlike prince, that he
granted an immunity to the earl and his followers. The parchment on which this
immunity was inscribed, is said to be still preserved in the archives of the Earls of
Caithness, and is marked with the drum-strings, having been cut out of a drum-head,
as no other parchment could be found in the army. The earl and his gallant band
perished to a man in the battle of Flodden ; since which period, it has been reckoned
unlucky in Caithness to *wear green*, or *cross the Ord on a Monday*, the day of the
week on which the chieftain advanced into Sutherland."

Leyden's *Poems.* Kelso, 1858. p. 298.

fore, they were very friendly;[5] for Surrey was commissioned to convey to him his royal bride, and the earl witnessed all the pageantry and festivity both before and after that joyous occasion, while his countess, on the day after the marriage, was presented with "xv elne claith of gold, quhen sche and her dochter, Lady Gray, clippit the king's berde." Still, it may have been in his public capacity alone that Surrey acted as he did, and if so, justice on his part was the less tempered with mercy. Viewing him in this light, he was so bent upon his duty of repelling assault, that no previous intimacy with an adversary, could avert in any degree his intended blow. Successful by his first epistle to the king in turning the bravery of the latter to his own hostile purpose, and learning on the return of Rouge Croix that the Scottish camp was removed to the hill of Flodden, a place admirable for defence, he again, by advice of his council, wrote to the king, to induce him, if possible, to descend from his position, which, he observed, resembled a fortress, and fight on Millfield Plain, which lay directly between the two armies. The missive was dated from Wooler-haugh, on the 7th September, at five o'clock in the afternoon, and signed by Surrey and eighteen of the principal men of the army. But the herald who conveyed it was not admitted to the royal presence, and the reply was, that it became not an earl to write in that way to a king; only no *sorcery* should be used, and no dependance was placed on any ground When the messenger-at-arms returned to Wooler-haugh early on Thursday the 8th, and shewed how the king would not abandon his place, another plan was devised. The English began to experience the want of provisions, for it would seem they brought none with them, and every article of food in the district before them had been prudently removed, lest it should be taken or destroyed by the enemy. Something effective, therefore, was necessary to be done, and by arrangement of Surrey and his council, the whole force advanced forward to the North, crossing the Till, and marching by Doddington, till they reached Barmoor Wood, about five miles north-east of Flodden, where they encamped for the night. East of Ford is a ridge of hills, from the highest point of which Lord Howard, the admiral, carefully observed the position of the Scottish army. On the evening of the same day, it was concluded to march again across the

---

[5] Soon after Queen Margaret's arrival in Edinburgh, she thus wrote to her father, Henry VII.:—
" My lorde of Surrey ys yn great favor with the Kyng her, that he cannott forber the companey of hym no tyme off the day. He and the bichopp off Murrey ordereth every thyng as nycht as they can to the Kyng's pleasur."
Ellis's *Letters*, First series, i., 42.

Till, not far from its confluence with the Tweed, and give battle to the enemy.

Next morning early, being Friday, the memorable 9th of September, in accordance with the said resolution, the English army were in motion, and instead of keeping the way direct to Berwick, they swerved to the north-west by Duddo, advancing between King James and his own land. At this time, Giles Musgrave, an Englishman, who was with the Scots and in favour with the king, endeavoured, though ineffectually, for the benefit of his own country, to persuade him to descend from Flodden, under pretence that Surrey was on his way, to waste and plunder Scotland. But the vanguard under command of Lord Howard, with the artillery, and stores consisting of baggage and ammunition, crossed the Till about eleven o'clock, at Twysel bridge, which is still remaining. The rearward, with its commander, the Earl of Surrey, also passed that stream about a mile higher up, at a place then called Millford, probably a ford near the mill of Heton, sufficiently shallow for the main body to pass over. Nearly all our historians blame King James for not attacking the English when they crossed the river, which, they relate, he might have done with great advantage, but Twysel is at a distance of about five miles from Flodden, and the king would not then abandon his favourable position.

Both the nobles and people of Scotland, being averse to the inroad, were opposed to war, and ere they left home, had all heard of the several warnings given to the nation, not to hold out mortal defiance to England. Even now, trifles had occurred to make them dread the worst, and almost every circumstance tended to lessen the assurance of a fortunate issue to the combat in which they were about to engage. In a council held by the king and his chief men, a hare started up among them, and though many a hand was lifted against the timid animal, it escaped through the whole army. The cloth of the royal tent, on the morning of the battle, was wet with moisture of a red colour, and mice had gnawed asunder the leathern strap which fastened the king's helmet. Still more, Friday from time immemorial was considered an unpropitious day, and now an event was to be decided thereon, upon which depended the destinies of a kingdom. All joyous sounds and lovely lineaments of the year had passed away. The very sky, we may suppose, was cloudy, for a south-east wind played mournfully among the trees, the leaves of which had lost the bright hue of summer, while the long grass, drenched with rain, waved sadly above the damp soil. Patches of cultured fields, few in number, had been stripped of the season's growth, and this the Scots had wasted and destroyed. The very face of nature was in the course of being changed, and many of themselves, as the hour of battle was at hand, would be swept away by the strong arm of the avenging foe.

When the English army emerged from the banks of the Till, and proceeded between King James and Scotland, their movement could not fail to cause great excitement among the Scots. Had they come either by the plain of Millfield or by Ford bridge, the king was ready to give them battle, but he had not anticipated any attack from the north. Could it be that the Earl of Surrey intended to assault him in his entrenchments, or did he mean to take possession of the neighbouring eminence, upwards of a mile to the west, called Branxton hill? The latter was evidently that leader's design, for the banners of his army moved on in that direction, and if he obtained such a position, he would not only annoy those in the camp, by cutting off all communication between them and Scotland, but meet them in battle at his pleasure on ground equal, if not superior, to that which they themselves occupied. The king, therefore, considering it would detract from his honour were he to remain still, as if beseiged in a fortress, or trust more to the strength of the ground he held than to the bravery of his people, resolved to quit Flodden, and occupy Branxton hill before it could be secured by the English. This was immediately carried into effect. The artillery, comprising seven beautiful culverins, founded by Robert Borthwick, and named the "Seven Sisters," were sent off first, the fighting men, in battle array, followed, with the king and his nobility on horseback near them ; the spoil and provisions were speedily removed, and fire being applied to the litter and refuse left behind, the smoke thereof, borne by the wind, floated densely away between the two armies.

During the two previous days the English had little else than water to drink, and on the day of conflict they had scarcely any food to eat, yet encouraged by the Earl of Surrey, who desired that they should acquit themselves like Englishmen, they advanced towards Branxton in regular order. At that hour it must have been a thrilling sight to witness such an host of determined men marching towards the Scots, with flags and pennons innumerable of every form and device floating above them, prepared to do battle in defence of their country. They were separated into two bodies or wards, nearly equal in number, each having a centre and a right and left wing—the foreward being on the right, and the rear or main-ward on the left. The former was commanded by Lord Thomas Howard, the admiral, with Henry Lord Clifford, usually called " the Shepherd Lord," aged sixty, Richard Nevill Lord Latimer, Lord Scrope of Upsal, Sir Christopher Ward, Sir John Everingham, Sir

Nicholas Appleyard, Sir William Sydney of Penshurst, Thomas Lord Conyers of Sockburn, John Lord Lumley, William Baron of Hylton, Sir William Bulmer and others, being the power of the Bishoprick under the banner of Saint Cuthbert, Robert Lord Ogle, Sir William Gascoigne the elder of Leasingcroft, Sir John Gower, and divers other gentlemen of Yorkshire and Northumberland, with their tenants and followers, also the mariners brought by the admiral himself, the whole amounting to about nine thousand men. Westward of the foreward, but near to it, was the extreme right wing under Sir Edmund Howard, brother to the admiral, and Marshall of the host, with whom were Sir Bryan Tunstall and one hundred men, Sir Thomas Butler of Beausey, Sir John Bothe, Sir John Lawrence of Dun, Sir Richard Bold with his vassals and archers from Lancashire, Sir Richard Cholmondeley of Cheshire, Sir John Bigot, Sir Thomas Fitz-William, Sir Robert Warcop, the men of Hull, the king's tenants of Hatfield, many from Lancashire and the county palatine of Chester, and two hundred men from the south of England, numbering altogether above three thousand. East of the Admiral's battalion was his left wing, under charge of Sir Marmaduke Constable of Flamburgh, who was seventy years of age, William Constable, his brother, Sir Robert, Marmaduke, and William, his sons, Sir William Percy, his son in law, with a large number of retainers of his brother, Earl Percy, Sir John Constable, others from Yorkshire and Northumberland, and all their respective followers, together with one thousand men from Lancashire, almost approaching in number to those who formed the right wing. Such was the foreward, and it was considerably in advance of the other portion of the army.

The centre of the rearward was commanded by the Earl of Surrey, in company with Sir Philip Tylney, Henry Lord Scrope of Bolton, Sir John Radcliffe of Lancashire, Sir George Dacre, Christopher Pickering, George Darcy, Sir Richard Tempest, Sir John Mandeville, Sir Christopher Clapham, William Gascoigne the younger, Bryan Stapleton, John Willoughby, John Stanley with the Bishop of Ely's servants, Sir Lionel Percy with an hundred followers and the Abbot of Whitby's tenants, the citizens of York and others, with their retainers, numbering, as records tell us, about five thousand men. Westward of Surrey, forming his right wing, though placed somewhere behind the other divisions, that assistance might be rendered when required, was Lord Dacre with fifteen hundred horse, the bowmen of Kendal wearing milk-white coats and red crosses, and the men of Keswick, Stanmore, Alston Moor, and Gilsland, chiefly bearing large bills. In company with Dacre was the Bastard Heron, commanding another troop of horse, trained to

ENGLISH ARMY.

Rear Ward

Fore Ward

Horse.
Lord Dacre.

Earl of Surrey.

Lord Thomas Howard.

Sir M. Constable.

Edmund Howard.

Huntley and Home.

Craw[f]ord and Montrose.

Horse.

Bothwell.

The King

Lennox and Argyle.

SCOTTISH ARMY.

Arrangement of Troops
at the Commencement of
The Battle of Flodden.

Border depredation, and ready at any time for battle. On the eastern edge of the field, forming Surrey's left wing, was a numerous division, both of horse and foot, headed by Sir Edward Stanley, a knight whose father having married the mother of Henry VII., brought him into close relationship with the king. Saving Sir William Molyneux of Seftonhall, in Cheshire, and Sir Henry Kickley, it is difficult to glean from our chronicles who were his gallant companions in arms, but his own son of the same name bore his banner, and his influence being extensive, he commanded the chief power of Cheshire and Lancashire—men well adapted for war, and exceedingly dexterous in the use of the bill and long bow. We have no direct information of the numbers contained in these two wings, but computing them at a low average, if upwards of three thousand be assigned to Stanley, and less than that amount to Lord Dacre, we shall probably be not far from the truth, for the force of the former, occupying the whole eastern side of the battle field, is estimated to have been the greater. These numbers, be it remembered, are in accordance with statements supplied by English writers who lived at or near that period, and whose narratives were published during the lifetime of many of the Flodden heroes.[6]

Unfortunately we have no authority, either from the English or Scottish historians, on which reliance can be placed, for ascertaining precisely the numbers of the Scottish army. Judging, however, from the desertions which took place day and night from the camp, four or five days previously—the eagerness of Surrey for battle, who we may suppose well knew what power he had to encounter—the desire of the Scottish nobles to withdraw over the Tweed, and the final result of the conflict, we would say the whole force at the king's disposal did not exceed from twenty to twenty-four thousand fighting men. It is said the Scottish nobles were desirous that the king should retire, and remain as a spectator aloof from danger, and then, however the fortune of the day went, his life would be preserved for the welfare of his country. They proposed the forces of the north should be led on by the Earls of Huntley, Argyle and Crawford; those of the west, by the Earl of Glen-

---

[6] See a tract of four leaves comprising a sketch of the battle, reprinted in 1809, under revise of Haslewood, and sold by R. Triphook. In 1822, it was added to the publications of the Typographical Society of Newcastle-upon-Tyne. The original had been emprinted by Richard Faques, shortly after the encounter; but from the incoherence of the sentence at which the second leaf ends and the third begins, though the catch-word "say-de" agrees, one leaf or more may have been wanting. The best and most ample account of the conflict, however, is found in Hall's *Chronicle*, an edition of which was published in 1550, four years before the demise of Thomas Lord Howard, the admiral, who, after the death of his father, became third Duke of Norfolk.

cairn and the Lords Graham and Maxwell; and the strength of the
south, by the Earls of Angus, Bothwell, and the Lord Home. But the
king would not listen to any arrangement of that kind, and hence it
was rejected. Indeed, from the leaders themselves being inexperienced
in every plan relating to open-field warfare, and participating in the
universal excitement caused by the rapidity with which they were at last
assailed, it is probable that the troops were not arranged in the most ap-
proved manner to withstand and vanquish an opposing army. They were
divided into five battalions, each numbering probably from four to five
thousand, the king himself heading that in the centre, whereby he was
supported by two wings on every side. Four of these divisions occupied
the whole front of Branxton hill, looking to the north, and ranging in lines
from west to east, with the artillery placed both before each body of men
and in the open spaces between them. That which remained, forming the fifth, was placed behind the king on his right, and leaned towards the rear of that on the eastern side of the field. Farthest to the
west was the extreme left wing, under Alexander Earl of Huntley and the
Lord Home—the former commanding Highlanders from Aberdeenshire
and other places, and the latter, being Warden of the Marches, guiding the
fierce Borderers, who were inured, from boyhood, to the strife and commotion of war. Next was another division from the central part of the Low-
lands and from Forfarshire, north of the entrance to the Firth of Tay,
under charge of John Earl of Crawford and William Earl of Montrose.
The third, towards the east, being the main body, was commanded by the
king himself, the principal men of the Church, and the nobility, with the
gentry, many of whom fought like common soldiers, and the whole com-
prised the very best and bravest warriors of Scotland. Eastward again,
in front, was the extreme right wing of the Scottish army, strong in
numbers, but consisting chiefly of undisciplined mountaineers from the
west of Scotland and the Isles, led on by Matthew Earl of Lennox and
Archibald Earl of Argyle. The last battalion, already alluded to, consisted
chiefly of yeomen and others from the Lothians, with the burghers of
the larger towns on the coast, under the guidance of Hepburn Earl of
Bothwell. This was a division of reserve stationed to yield help where
it was requisite, but more especially to wait upon and succour the king.
Flags and pennons of every kind, more than could be counted, waved
and fluttered in the wind; and we may suppose that near the centre of
the whole floated the royal banner of Scotland, borne by Sir Adam Forman, with the well known bearings upon it, chiefly in gold. But for all
this display, the warriors who composed the army, knowing they ought
not to have been there, grasped their weapons with a hesitating hand.

It was not for Freedom, or to roll back the tide of Oppression, that they were about to join in battle. They had been led to the field by the king; but, actuated by no lofty or patriotic aim, they occupied their position more in self-defence, than with the stern determination to meet, and, if possible, to overcome their enemy.

During the advance of the English, the smoke floating away to the north-west from the deserted camp, completely concealed the armies from each other. The day was now far spent, but Lord Howard's troops with his right and left wings, accompanied by the artillery, and directed onward by able guides, still led the way. Natural wood at that time skirted all the lower parts of the valley, at the bottom of which was a morass of considerable length, where the slender stream of Pallinsburn now flows, and when the Admiral with his forces crossed a small brook there named Sandyford, which a man might step over, the smoke had cleared away, and the divisions of the Scottish army, some square and some in the form of a wedge, were observed near at hand, with long spears and banners displayed, extending along the whole northern brow of the hill. Unable himself, with the forces he commanded, to encounter the foe with any reasonable hope of success, the admiral halted, and, taking the *Agnus Dei* which hung at his breast, he sent it to his father, with a request that in all haste he would advance to the conflict. Speedily the Earl came up with the rearward, until the battalions, though within a bow-shot apart, were nearly in a line with each other, and then they moved together onward with their faces to the south, the artillery being still placed in due order before and between the columns. At length, on arriving within range, the guns on both sides opened fire. The Scottish cannon, standing on ground so high above the masses of men at whom they were pointed, and being without any support save their own weight in the recoil, shot over the heads of the English, doing little or no injury; while those of England were discharged with such precision that the chief-gunner slew the master of the Scottish ordnance, beating off the men from their guns, and killing many in the ranks. When, however, the opposing squadrons successively approached and confronted each other closely, the firing was gradually discontinued.

As the English advanced onward, circling the western base of Branxton hill, that they might enter into close battle, Sir Bryan Tunstall took up mould from the ground and put it into his mouth in token of his mortality. He was in the wing of the foreward under Sir Edmund Howard, and between four and five o'clock in the afternoon that leader's division, having ascended the western acclivity of the hill, was the first to encounter the left wing of the Scots led on by Huntley and Home. The attack of the Highlanders with swords and axes, and the Borderers with levelled spears, was fierce and terrific. The Marshall endeavoured, however, to withstand the onset bravely, and his exertions were ably supported, but having under him a large number of men from Cheshire, who were jealous of the power of the Howards, and much attached to the house of Stanley, these with several from Lancashire and Yorkshire, when they were met by the Scots, unhappily turned their backs and fled, whereupon Tunstall was slain, and the other warriors, who formed the wing, were placed in the most imminent danger. They wavered for a time, but the valour of Scotland prevailed, for Sir Edmund Howard, though cased in complete steel, was three several times felled to the ground, his division was speedily put to flight, and many prisoners taken. This was performed almost in full view of both armies, while the Bastard Heron, though sore wounded, for the adjoining English and Scottish wings had already joined battle, came with his outlaws to the leader's rescue, and Lord Dacre, with his horse and bowmen, arrived in time to check the impetuosity of the Scots, killing several friends of Lord Home and others—not, however, without injury to his own party, for his brother Sir Philip was taken prisoner and many of his adherents slain.

When the conflict began, the position of the King's army was admirable, for he had an advantage highly essential to success in military evolutions, which great generals cannot always procure—that of causing his enemy to fight him on ground of his own selection. Defective as his strength might be in point of numbers, had he remained where he was, maintaining his position, and making his battalions keep their place till encountered foot to foot by the foe—then regulating their movements as occasion required—every chance was in his favour for victory. But the great defect in his character, a blind and somewhat romantic attachment to what he conceived to be high honour and chivalric principles, again became apparent, and he imprudently threw away the privilege he held on a hazard of very doubtful issue. Possessing also, to a remarkable degree, the power of kindling those around him with his own heroic energy, he had the utmost confidence that every man under his sway would exert himself to the utmost for the honour of Scotland. Moreover, in his reply to Surrey, he had avowed his contempt for any advantage of ground : upon this he had acted on quitting Flodden, and now the English cannon galled his ranks, while his own artillery, deserted by the gunners, could not repay the enemy's fire with anything like effect. Having likewise witnessed the bravery of his left wing, headed by Huntley and the Chamberlain—for the struggle there was yet undecided—and obeying the impulse of his own sanguine temperament, he dismounted from his horse, and commanding the chief nobility and gentry around him to do the same, he advanced with his division against the enemy. The next battalion, under Crawford and Montrose, and also that of Bothwell, accompanied him—the former on his left being in advance, and the latter partly behind to the right, still retaining its distance from his own. This lack of prudence on the part of the king—for again he opposed the advice of his council—amazed every one near him, and his steadiest friends regarded each other with perplexity, as if conscious they were wilfully throwing away their chance of victory. It was customary to meet an enemy in battle with the clang of trumpets, and the shouts of the slogans of the several leaders; but in this instance, King James moved slowly down the front of Branxton hill with his battalions in perfect and regular order, as if intent only upon the desperate purpose before him, without making the slightest noise.

When the Scottish warriors of the left wing were engaged with their opponents, the main division of the English foreward, under Lord Thomas Howard, consisting, as has been said, of his mariners, the strength of Durham, and others of Northumberland, &c., was the next to join battle, near the foot of the hill, with the opposite battalion of Scots who descended before the king, under the Earls of Crawford and Montrose. Here the English considerably outnumbered the foe, and their large bills and axes were brought into terrible collision with the bristling lines of levelled spears handled by the Scottish soldiers. The men of Northumberland and Durham were more accustomed to the pressure of conflict than their enemies, who had been reared chiefly towards the centre of Scotland, and the struggle was most obstinate and bloody. The admiral was ultimately joined by his brother, Sir Edmund Howard, who, after his own men were scattered, and he himself escaped, drew off eastward to the main body of the foreward, and on his way met and killed Sir David Home. Lord Howard, in all probability, was also assisted by the warriors forming his left wing, under Sir Marmaduke Constable and his kinsmen, for our historians mention no body of Scots with whom the aged knight fought, but there can be no doubt that with his brave followers, he performed an active part in the battle, on behalf of his country. So fierce did the struggle continue, that the Scots at length perceived it was with great difficulty they could maintain their ground. Gordon Earl of Huntly, and Lord Home, after dispersing the English right wing, rendered at the time no further assistance to their neighbours, but remained aloof with their troops, as if to keep Lord Dacre in check, guarding the prisoners they had taken, and watching the progress of events in the field before them.

Still farther east, the king's division, being chiefly tall goodly men, and all on foot, with long spears, had entered into battle with the front of the English rearward, commanded by the Earl of Surrey. In descending the hill, they were exposed to a tremendous shower of arrows from the English ranks, but as they generally wore plate armour, only a very few were wounded or slain. During their advance, the spearmen took the precaution to throw off their boots or shoes, and, thus disencumbered, acquitted themselves with the most heroic bravery. When the spears failed, sternly and silently they drew their large and sharp swords, and used them with terrible effect. The shock when both sides met was dreadful, for the Scots advancing fiercely with lines of serried spears, encountered an insurmountable barrier of large bills, wielded by powerful yeomen, which hewed them down, despite their panoply of steel, crashing buckler, helm, breastplate, and mail, with fearful strokes. Lances were cut asunder or struck aside, and blow after blow dashed the spearmen to the ground. Neither did the bravery of the English, nor the defensive armour they wore, sustain them unscathed in the heat of the encounter, for it is recorded that the northern spear was even more fatal than the southern axe and bill. Here was no shifting—no attempt of a single soldier to fly—but onward and forward came rank after rank, performing what man could achieve in terrible and most deadly conflict.

It is said the troops composing the right wing of the Scottish army— the Campbells, Macleans, and other hardy clans, upon the east side of the battle field, under the Earls of Lennox and Argyle—who up to this time kept the hill, on perceiving before them how the central division, and that of Hepburn Earl of Bothwell, with the king and nobility, were engaged with Surrey's main battalion, attempted to succour their countrymen, but were instantly attacked by Sir Edward Stanley's archers of Cheshire and Lancashire, who were the last to enter into battle. The English of this division were numerous; and the bowmen directing their long shafts with unerring force into the masses of Highlanders and Islesmen on the slope above them, the ranks of the mountaineers were broken, and they rushed down, axe and claymore in hand, upon their assailants, in spite of the peremptory orders of their commanders and the earnest entreaties of La Motte, the ambassador of France. But the front of Stanley's force, consisting of a large proportion of bill-men, stood firm, repelling like a rock the ocean fury of the wild northmen. In this onset, as the Scots had few or no spears to defend themselves from cavalry, their confusion was increased by a sudden attack in flank of three companies of men-at-arms, who were

watching an opportunity to assist their countrymen. By this unex-
pected movement the courageous Highlanders were overthrown, and
such as hewed a way through their opponents, dispersed and saved themselves by escaping to the woods below. In accomplishing this successful
measure, Stanley, with his brave yeomen, conscious of their superiority,
advanced upward against the enemy, killing Argyle, Lennox, and La
Motte, and overcoming every opposing obstacle till they reached the
higher part of the hill. All this time the deadly strife between the divisions of King James and that of the Earl of Surrey continued unabated,
whereupon Stanley, turning his forces round to the right, and advancing
downward in a northern direction, passed over the place where the
king's battle first commenced, and closed in upon the right flank of the
Scots, who still kept their ground with most desperate resolution.

The shadows of evening were now settling quietly down over hill
and valley, while the Lord Admiral's men to the south-west were equally
successful with those of Stanley in vanquishing their enemies and putting them to flight. The Scottish leaders, Montrose and Crawford,
charging on foot to encourage their wavering ranks against superior
numbers, fell under the English weapons. Few prisoners were taken,
but many men were killed, and the whole were completely discomfited.
Having thus cleared the ground before him, the admiral now turned
round to the north-east, and, acting as if in concert with Stanley, charged
the left side of the Scottish squadron, the warriors of which still held their
place around the king. When the latter brave body of heroic men were
previously joined by the reserve under the Earl of Bothwell, consisting of
the Lothian yeomanry, such was the onslaught, that the standard of Surrey was in imminent danger of being either taken or beaten down. But
now the English bill made great slaughter among the nobility of Scotland.
It has been mentioned, that when Archibald Earl of Angus quitted the
camp he left behind him his two eldest sons in token of his fidelity to the
king. These were George Master of Angus and Sir William of Glenbervy,
both of whom were slain. Among other instances, Robert Lord Keith
and William de Keith, the eldest sons also of William Keith Earl of Marishall, fell in the conflict.[7] The Scots, however, fought like men who

[7] The standard of William Earl of Marishall, which is preserved in the Advocates'
Library at Edinburgh, is almost the only relic of the battle which has escaped the
ravages of time, and come down to our own day. The bearer of it was called Black
John Skirving of Plewland Hill. Besides the property of that name, which lies in
the parish of Humbie, East Lothian, he had four adjoining acres of the land of Keith
Marishall, for carrying the standard. Skirving, on perceiving the unhappy termina-
tion of the fight for his own people, tore the flag from the staff, and concealed it about
his person, before surrendering himself a prisoner to the conquerors. After his release,
the relic remained in possession of his family for many generations, until a descend-

had formed the resolution either to win the field, or yield up their lives for the cause of their king. Still the forces under the Earl of Surrey, despite the resolute attempts of Scottish prowess to break through their ranks, kept together, and firmly maintained their footing. So fierce indeed was the encounter, that each party being aroused to vengeance by the "cruel fighting" of their opponents, no quarter was given on either side.

From the time that Lord Home, with his Borderers united with Huntley in repelling the forces of Sir Edmund Howard, he remained on the hill-side with his troops, without again entering into battle. Huntley, on perceiving how much his sovereign required assistance, prepared to render it, and asked Home to accompany him on that duty, when the latter observed, "the man does well this day who saves himself: we fought those who were opposed to us and beat them; let our other companies do the same!" Huntley, however, not discouraged by this reply, attempted to succour the king, and closed again with the southern host, encountering, it is said, Stanley's division[8]; but perceiving the gallant squadron who fought with King James completely surrounded by the English, and seeing his aid to be ineffectual in rescuing his countrymen, he withdrew his followers from the strife, and was one of the few leaders who was fortunate enough to escape. The struggle was now dreadful, for Lord Dacre, observing that Home's Borderers were not likely to give him annoyance, brought round his mounted array of lances, and charged the royal division in the rear, thus closing up to this loyal and devoted band of heroes all chance of escape. Still, it is placed on record by one of our most valuable English chroniclers,[9] that if at this period,

ant, William Skirving, presented it to the noble institution above named. A copy of it is given in Weber's edition of the old Poem of the *Battle of Floddon Field*, Edinburgh, 1808. It is fringed all round, and appears to be of pale silk, blanched by time, with the motto "VERITAS VINCIT," and three stags' heads erased upon it in black. In length it is about four feet four inches, one foot six inches in depth at the staff end, and swallow-tailed, with the opening about ten inches up the standard.

[8] Weber, in his notes to the old Poem already mentioned, says that Huntley's standard was taken by a leader alluded to in a previous page—Sir William Molyneux, whose hall in Cheshire was long graced by the martial trophy. A drawing of it was made by the heralds in the time of Elizabeth, which is now deposited in the Heralds' College, and a copy is supplied in Weber's volume. That author observes the figures thereon, consisting of a hawk, a stag and hound, with ships, represent Huntley's armorial coat, with the motto, "*Clame tot*," otherwise "Let all repair to this pennon." There is doubt of such a standard being taken, but the bearings thereon are not those of Huntley. That earl's arms were the same as those of his father, the second earl, *namely :*—Quarterly; first, azure, three boars' heads couped or, for Gordon; second, or, three lions' heads erased gules, for Badenoch; third, or, three crescents within a double tressure flowered and counterflowered gules, for Seaton; fourth, azure, three cinquefoils argent, for Fraser; crest, on a helmet with mantlings, a stag's head.

[9] Hollinshead's History of Scotland, ed. 1585, p. 301.

Home, and the remainder of the king's army, had assailed the English, who were now all collected together, "victory had undoubtedly rested with the Scots." We have thereby proof that the strength of England was almost exhausted, and her warriors knew this so well that afterwards they "confessed themselves bound to God for their safety and deliverance out of that danger." All hope for Scotland being thus thrown away, night advanced as if to extend her dusky mantle over the battle field, in compassion for the appalling waste thereon of human life. The carnage was indeed awful, for the archers continued to pour into the centre their arrowy showers, and the bill-men plied their terrible blades upon the Scots with a force and dexterity that no armour could withstand. According to the vivid lines in *Marmion* :—

> "The English shafts in volleys hail'd,
> In headlong charge their horse assail'd ,
> Front, flank, and rear, the squadrons sweep
> To break the Scottish circle deep,
>   That fought around their king.
> But yet, though thick the shafts as snow,
> Though charging knights like whirlwinds go,
> Though bill-men ply the ghastly blow,
>   Unbroken was the ring ;
> The stubborn spearmen still made good
> Their dark impenetrable wood,
> Each stepping where his comrade stood,
>   The instant that he fell.
> No thought was there of dastard flight ;
> Link'd in the serried phalanx tight,
> Groom fought like noble, squire like knight,
>   As fearlessly and well ;
> Till utter darkness closed her wing
> O'er their thin host and wounded King.
> Then skilful Surrey's sage commands
> Led back from strife his shatter'd bands ;
>   And from the charge they drew,
> As mountain-waves from wasted lands
>   Sweep back to ocean blue.
> Then did their loss his foemen know ;
> Their King, their Lords, their mightiest low,
> They melted from the field as snow,
> When streams are swoln and south winds blow,
>   Dissolves in silent dew.
> Tweed's echoes heard the ceaseless plash,
>   While many a broken band,
> Disorder'd though her currents dash,
>   To gain the Scottish land—

> To town and tower, to down and dale,
> To tell red Flodden's dismal tale,
> And raise the universal wail.
> Tradition, legend, tune, and song,
> Shall many an age that wail prolong:
> Still from the sire the son shall hear
> Of the sad strife, and carnage drear,
>   Of Flodden's fatal field,
> Where shiver'd was fair Scotland's spear,
>   And broken was her shield!"

North of Crookham West Field, adjoining a fence, and within a short arrow-flight from the road, on a gentle elevation, stands an upright block of unhewn stone upwards of a yard in diameter, and nearly seven feet high. Some writers say that the Earl of Surrey caused this stone to be set up as a memorial that the battle was won; but there is a probability that it stood in its present position previous to the sixteenth century, and that it had been used as a gathering point to the forces of England,[10] when they were about to cross the march and waste the Scottish Borders. If so, it is not unlikely that Surrey passed it on his way to battle, and to this spot in the twilight, the aged leader, who was still uncertain of the result of the deadly conflict, withdrew the remainder of his wearied forces to remain till the morning. But amid the dead and dying—it being an awful night for thousands—the thieves of Tyndale and Teviotdale, with other Borderers, continued to pursue their avocation with great alacrity, spoiling the slain over the whole field, rifling the contents of the pavilions, and taking away horses in vast numbers wherever they were found. Almost every one spoke evil of Lord Home, who, for the manner in which he had conducted himself towards the

---

[10] It answered this purpose thirty-two years after the battle of Flodden, and was called "The Standing Stone on Crookham Moor," though in the present day it is named "The King's Stone." In "A Contemporary Account of the Earl of Hertford's Second Expedition to Scotland, and of the Ravages committed by the English Forces in September, 1545," from a manuscript in Trinity College Library, Dublin, edited by David Laing, Esq., F.S.A. Scot., and printed in the Transactions of the Society of which he is so valuable a member, vol. i. pp. 272-3, the following passage occurs:—

"The Erle of Harford departhit from Nywcastell the 5 day of Settember; and all his armey had a day a pointit to mytte att the Stannyngston* vpon Crocke a More,† the 8 day of thes present, & all the caryadge and ordenannce and monyssion: and so the dyd: the said Erle rod from Nywcastell to Anwicke a Satherday, and their he rest Sonday; and a Monday to Cheidyngham;‡ and a Tywsseday to the forsaid Ston on Crackamowre, and past fart'‖ a myll, and their campet; and a Wenesday past by Warke, and so a longs the water in iij batelles,§ and so past the furd w^t the foreward and the most part of the battaill and their ordenannce."

* Standingstone. † Crookham Moor. ‡ Chillingham.
‖ further. § companies, battalions.

close of the battle, and in bringing off unscathed a very large number of his followers, was regarded as a traitor to his country.

When the light of day came, the Earl of Surrey ascertained that the chief portion of the Scottish army who survived, conscious of their loss, had abandoned the field. But a number of them appearing on a hill, and endangering the safety of Lord Howard, who was near, Sir William Blacknall ordered some of the artillery to be discharged upon them, when they departed. Surrey now gave thanks to God for the success of the arms of England;[11] and calling around him such of his principal leaders as had distinguished themselves, he created forty knights, among whom were his own son, Sir Edmund Howard, Lord Scrope of Upsal, Sir William Percy, Sir Christopher Dacre, Sir Marmaduke Constable the younger, Sir George Darcy, Sir William Gascoigne the younger, Sir John Stanley, Sir Bryan Stapleton, Sir Ralph Bowes of Streatlam, Sir Roger of Fenwick, Sir George Grey of Horton, Sir Thomas Conyers, the Lord Ogle, and the Lord Lumley. Then he appointed Sir Philip Tylney, the company of the Admiral, the retinue of Lord Scrope of Bolton, the Lord Latimer, Sir Marmaduke Constable, Sir William Percy, Sir Nicholas Appleyard, and their companies, to keep the field, that the artillery of Scotland might be preserved, and the whole number of pieces were conveyed, by Lord Dacre's assistance, to the castle of Etal. An account of the battle was then written in French, either by Lord Thomas Howard, or probably under his directions, and sent to the King of England. The chief men who contributed to earn the victory, now prepared to return home. Surrey had received instructions from his royal master to act only on the defensive against Scotland, but he had another cause for not wounding her deeper by more effusion of blood. No arrangement had been made for victualling his forces, and besides, they were so reduced as to be incapable of bestowing upon her any great

[11] For his good fortune in gaining the victory, Surrey was created Duke of Norfolk on the 1st Feb. 1514. On the bend which appeared in the Howard arms was added an augmentation of the upper part of a red lion, depicted in the same way as that in the arms of Scotland, and pierced through the mouth with an arrow. Hollinshead mentions also, that after the fight at Flodden, the earl gave to his servants the cognizance of the white lion (descended to him from the Mowbrays) standing over the red lion of Scotland, and tearing it with his paws. This they were to wear on their left arms. He died in 1524. His son and heir, Lord Thomas the Admiral, succeeded him in the earldom of Surrey, and on Norfolk's disease, he came also to the dukedom. Towards the close of his days he was unfortunate, for being attainted in 1546, and condemned to suffer death, his life was saved by Henry VIII. dying on the night previous to the time appointed for his execution. He was restored again to his honours in 1553, but died in the following year. His son and heir, Henry Howard Earl of Surrey, the poet—a gentle branch from such an austere stock—was also attainted and beheaded in 1547. The son and heir, again, of the poet, was restored in blood and honours in 1553, and succeeded to his grandfather's dignities in 1554, but was also attainted and beheaded in 1572, when his honours were forfeited.

additional amount of punishment. A great many horses were secured, and on searching the field, large quantities of provisions, consisting of wine, ale, beef, mutton, cheese, &c., were found in the Scottish camp.

Among the slain, on the side of Scotland, was a natural son of King James, an amiable young man, who was Archbishop of St. Andrews, with two bishops, two abbots, one dean, thirteen earls, fifteen lords and chiefs of clans, with La Motte the French Ambassador, who at the time was secretary to the King. The gentry who fell were numerous; for almost every family in the kingdom mourned the loss of one or two of its members, while in some instances the father and every son he had were killed.[12] The common people who were slain might number about eight thousand; but of this we have no positive proof, for all the bodies, both English and Scots, were entirely stripped of their apparel, and save for the beard, which the latter usually wore, and which was also, we may suppose, worn by many of the English people, those of one nation might readily be taken for those of another. The English might have upwards of five thousand killed, for the Scots fought with the utmost desperation even to the last, and it is generally admitted that the loss was heavy; but the honour of the victory made it be less felt, and the number slain, with few exceptions, consisted of the middle and lower classes. This proves most conclusively that those of the higher ranks had not exposed themselves much to the Scottish axe or spear, and that though the weather had been most unfavourable for the use of the long bow, yet the archers, the artillerymen, and especially the bill-men, had performed no mean part in securing the triumph of England.

The probability is, that King James lost his life on the battle field,[13] only it may be allowed us to examine the evidence given by our chroniclers in support of that event. Nearly all agree that when he saw his standard-bearer, Sir Adam Forman, fall, disdaining captivity, he pressed forward into the enemy's lines and was slain. On the day after the battle Lord Dacre discovered his body, surrounded by those of the nobility and others who had fallen near him, at about a spear's length from where the Earl of Surrey had stood. Several deadly wounds were inflicted thereon, especially one by an arrow, and another

---

[12] It is said that Andrew Pitcairn of Pitcairn, with seven sons, went to the battle, where they were all slain. One son, either born afterwards, or a child at the time, continued the family. The widow and boy, owing to the severity of the times, were turned out of possession of the inheritance, but James V. granted a charter, restoring her to her jointure, and the heir to his estate, mentioning that Pitcairn and seven sons fell at Flodden, fighting valiantly for his royal father.

[13] He left an infant son below two years of age, and from this scion of royalty we trace the descent of our own illustrious Queen.

by a bill which had opened the neck to the middle, while the left hand
was almost cut off in two places. Surrey, they say, sent the Queen of
England a piece of the coat-armour of the king; again, the body was
recognised at Berwick by Sir William Scott, Chancellor of Scotland, and
Sir John Forman, the King's sergeant-porter, both of whom were taken
prisoners. In opposition to these statements it may be observed, that
several officers, by the king's command, were arrayed similar to himself,
and Lord Elphinston resembled him in personal appearance very much ;
that it would be difficult to prove the body was found within a spear's
length from the Earl of Surrey, when the latter could not possibly be
stationary on the field ; that Lord Dacre may have been mistaken, and
the prisoners, apart from conviction, might have a motive for what they
said ; and also, that though a dispensation from the Pope was obtained
for the burial of King James in consecrated ground, that service was
never performed,[14] shewing as if doubts had arisen at head-quarters of
the body being that of the King. Moreover, from a State paper, dated
June 23, 1525, we learn that the Queen, who wished to be divorced
from the Earl of Angus, her second husband, observed, "she was married to the said earl, the King of Scots her husband being alive, and
that same King was living three years after the field of Flodden." The
iron chain which the King is said to have constantly worn, in remorse
for his share in the death of his father, could not be produced by the
English. In the College of Arms at London are deposited the sword and
dagger which are said to have belonged to him, having been gifted to
that institution by the Earl of Surrey himself. Are they the genuine
weapons of James IV. of Scotland, and can undoubted proof of such a
present be established ?[15]

[14] Stowe's own words on this historical episode, are valuable. They are supplied
from his *Survey of London*, 1618, p. 539.
   "After the battle the bodie of the said king, being found, was closed in lead, and
conveyed from thence to London, and to the monasterie of Sheyne, in Surry, where
it remained for a time, in what order I am not certaine ; but, since the dissolution of
that house, in the reign of Edward VI., Henry Gray, Duke of Norfolke, being lodged,
and keeping house there, I have been shewed the same bodie, so lapped in lead, close
to the head and bodie, throwne into a waste room, amongst the old timber, lead, and
other rubble. Since the which time, workmen there, for their foolish pleasure, hewed
off his head ; and Lancelot Young, master glazier to the Queen Elizabeth, feeling a
sweet savour to come from thence, and seeing the same dried from all moisture, and
yet the form remaining, with haire of the head, and beard red, brought it to London,
to his house in Wood-street, where, for a time, he kept it, for its sweetness, but in the
end, caused the sexton of that church (St Michael's, Wood-street) to bury it amongst
other bones taken out of their charnel."
[15] Many of the people of Scotland would not believe the king was slain, but deemed
he escaped, and that he was gone on a pilgrimage to the Holy Land, to atone for the
part he took in the death of his father, and his own errors. Others insisted that he
was seen alive, near Kelso, on the close of the day of battle, and a whisper prevailed

This was called the Battle of Flodden by the Scots, from their camp being a few days on that prominent position, and that of Branxton moor by the English, from having been fought to the south, near that village. As no memorial has been set up to mark the battle field, it seems desirable to glance over such evidence on this subject, as may enable us to ascertain the locality with some approximation to truth. By the tent shewn on Speed's Map of Northumberland, published in 1610, also by that of Blaeu, in 1646, who copied the former, and by several modern plans of the battle, we would suppose it had been stricken near to the farm-stead of Mardon. But by a most careful perusal of several original accounts of the battle by Hall and other early writers,[16] also by recent discoveries, and likewise by personal examination of the ground, ample authority exists for saying the general onslaught must have been made considerably to the west of that place. Our best historians agree that the king, making downward, encountered the English near the foot of the hill called Branxton. In the churchyard of that village, under the footpath, large quantites of bones, including those of horses, were discovered about a foot below the surface. On the low marshy ground near the source of Pallinsburn, a cannon ball of lead, weighing above thirteen pounds was found, and another of the same material was dug up west of Branxton hill. One of iron was also ploughed up near the

that he was murdered by a servant of the Lord Home. On the popular impression of this circumstance, I am indebted to my friend Mr. William Brockie, of South Shields, for the following particulars:—

"THE KING'S GRAVE.—A correspondent of the *Kelso Chronicle*, referring, in 1851, to a tradition he had heard his father and other aged people about Sprouston tell, in his youth, of a skeleton, found in the Berry Moss, near Kelso, with a gold chain about it, with links corresponding in number to the years of King James IV.'s age, mentions also a circumstance which he says had been related to him, about forty years before, by a very respectable farmer who lived in the immediate vicinity of Hume Castle. He goes on to say:—'Stitchell and Hume are conjoined parishes. The church of the latter is in ruins, but the churchyard still remains, and is still used as a place of interment. One day, when passing, my informant pointed to a small mound, which was called the King's Grave, or that of some distinguished person. It was customary, he said, from time immemorial, when a funeral entered the churchyard, to walk in procession round this grave, and return to the spot where the dead was to be buried, in whatever part of the churchyard that might be. One cold and stormy winter day, the procession was objected to by some of the parties in attendance, and from that time the practice was discontinued.' 'Might not,' he asks, ' the skeleton found in the Berry Moss, have been interred there, and hence the origin of this mark of reverence to the grave of royalty ?' "

[16] Lingard, in his *History*, fifth edition, 1849, iv. 371, enumerates four contemporary and detailed accounts of the battle. "One is by Hall, xlii.; a second equally minute but more elegant, by Giovio, the Italian Historian, l. xxi. f. 102 ; a third, formerly alluded to, by Lord Thomas Howard, preserved in the Heralds' Office, and published in Pinkerton's History, ii. App. 456 ; and a fourth printed by Galt, in the Appendix to his *Life of Wolsey*, p. 1." The last is the tract of four leaves mentioned in a preceding page. A letter from Queen Catherine to King Henry VIII., written after the battle, is printed in Ellis's *Letters*, First Series, i., 88.

church, and the sizes of all correspond to what we may conceive the calibre of guns would be in the early part of the sixteenth century. A French gold coin, dated about 1530, was turned up a few years ago on the undulating ground west of Branxton, lost probably by some pilgrim of France visiting the place where so much of Scotland's blood was shed by way of serving that kingdom. But the most convincing proof of the battle having been fought there, is that, about forty years ago, Mr. Andrew Rankin, a churchwarden of the parish, while in the act of cutting a drain through some mossy ground, near the western base of Branxton hill, opened a large pit of human bones at nearly three and a half feet below the surface. The direction of the drain lay from east to west, and the pit was several yards wide, but how far it extended from north to south, Mr. Rankin neglected to ascertain. Keeping these several matters in view, the probability is, that King James occupied, with the five divisions of his army, the whole northern front of the hill, his left wing extending to a small ravine, which descends to the north-west, and his right division reaching east of the road which leads from Branxton over the ridge to Flodden. Pallinsburn, at that time, almost from its source down to near Crookham, flowed through a bog or morass, and from the rain which fell previous to the battle, this would likely be under water; consequently, the chief portion of the army of England, in all probability, passed the valley near the source of that brook. The remainder might pass lower down, either by what was called "Branx Brig,"[17] a little to the north of Mardon, or near to Crookham, in which case they would join their countrymen at Branxton, which was formerly much larger than it is at present. Again, during the two or three hours when the battle was fought, a large number of horses, many tents and much baggage remained probably in and about the village. At a short distance to the south-west is a hill of moderate dimensions, a desirable spot for Surrey to occupy, which in former times may have been resorted to in the summer evenings by the piper of the place, who likely had his croft there; and if by the faint echo of some old tradition we could learn that the spot was once known as "Pipard Hill," such intelligence might enable the modern pilgrim to identify the spot where Scotland's King, after nobly bearing himself, weapon in hand, against opposing hosts, was slain. From this elevation, lines ranging to the east and the south-west, taking in the whole lower parts of Branxton hill, will circumscribe nearly the

[17] If this bridge was erected at the period when the battle was fought, it may have been that which the chief gunner of Scotland wished to destroy, as the English were passing over it, but was prevented by the king. Our historians who mention the incident—only they are evidently in error—say it was the bridge over Till.

ground whereon the battle was fought. An attempt by a fugitive body of Scots, either to strike a last blow upon the enemy, or to avail themselves of horses or spoil, in the open churchyard, where they would meet with opposition, will account for the quantity of bones found there. Other deposits of similar kind may yet be discovered, which will tend to fix the limits of the contest more accurately; but we may be assured that many who fell at no great distance from Branxton would likewise obtain Christian burial in its hallowed churchyard.

This was the greatest, the last, and the most decisive battle ever stricken on the Borders. England, though her loss was great, obtained thereby an ascendancy over her rival which stayed the contention of arms, and evinced she would not submit to be injured with impunity. To Scotland it was a most stunning and dreadful blow. The first of her clergy, nobility, and gentry, with the very best of her warriors, all yielded up their lives for the martial display and chivalric bearing of their gallant and beloved King. When the sad tidings reached city, town, and village, shrieks and outpourings of female anguish from palace, hall, bower, and cottage, were heard in every direction. Wives were made widows—mothers lost their sons—sisters were left brotherless—maids were bereaved of their lovers—and grief preying upon affectionate and susceptible hearts, would bring many a fair face to the grave, ere the following spring clothed the earth with beauty. It was not till nearly two succeeding generations passed away that Scotland regained her wonted cheerfulness; and even a century afterwards, when the direct descendant of the monarch, who lost all at Flodden, occupied the English throne, the story of that field—woeful as "The Dead March" in *Saul*—was listened to with regret. Later still, the mournful theme was taken up by her national bards, who instinctively tuned their harps to the tone of popular feeling; and the strains they have sung of that great disaster, accompanied by Tradition's wild but welcome tongue, will continue to be prized, while tenderness and heroic energy find an echo in the bosoms of her people.

Christmas Eve, 1818.

APPENDIX.

ILLUSTRATIONS.

WHEN the Society of Antiquaries of Newcastle-upon-Tyne met at Flodden Field, on Tuesday the 27th July, 1858, they received much attention from the Rev. Robert Jones of Branxton, to whom their best thanks were subsequently awarded. At that meeting it was suggested that a stone ought to be set up near the spot where Mr. Rankin discovered the pit of bones, and to Mr. Jones the Society are obliged for having respectfully made known the circumstance to John Collingwood, Esq., the proprietor of the ground, who in the most liberal manner undertook to erect, at his own expense, a memorial on the spot, to commemorate the solitary grave of so many of the Flodden heroes. To Mr. Jones also the writer is indebted for an original draught of the map, whence that which accompanies the foregoing paper has been reduced and engraved. By residing almost upon the battle field, and being well acquainted with the whole district, Mr. Jones has likewise been enabled to collect information from the aged people in the neighbourhood respecting the battle, and the probable way through which the English army advanced to the field, which he freely communicated, and of which some use has been made in the previous paper. On this subject, or any other connected with the history of the battle, as the writer has no theory to support, and no other aim than the elucidation of truth, he considers it an act of justice to his readers to lay before them the observations of that gentleman at length, reserving to himself the exercise of his own deliberate judgment. All the light which can be thrown upon a celebrated event in history is acceptable; hence the communication forms an appropriate accompaniment to what has been already related.

"Branxton Vicarage, 6th Nov. 1858.

"MY DEAR SIR,—Since sending you a plan of the Battle Field of Flodden, I have made all the research I possibly could for information respecting the advance of Surrey's army, after crossing the Till at Twizel Bridge and Heaton Ford. I have inspected the ground he would have to march over, and have made all the enquiry I could from the oldest people in my parish, who have resided therein from infancy, and whose ancestors for generations past, have been brought up in the immediate neighbourhood of Flodden Field. The result of this research and enquiry, I now feel great pleasure in submitting for your perusal, and I trust approval, being fully persuaded that any information I could give on the subject you are at present so laudably engaged in, will be acceptably and friendly received.

"Mr. Rankin, my churchwarden, the old man you saw when the Newcastle Antiquarian Society visited the field last summer, has given me some very important information, and which may elucidate a very important fact relative to the approach to Branxton of one part of Surrey's army, which crossed the Ford at Heaton Mill. I have in my map traced the small burn called Pallinsburn, situated to the north of my parish, which runs to the south of Crookham, and empties itself into the Till a little below that village. I am firmly persuaded that the source of this burn, at the time of the battle, took its rise from a very swampy part of land, which is called the bog, and which extended from the road leading to Coldstream to the foot of the hill, by the Blue Bell, a distance of rather more than a mile. This bog was impassable in many parts when I first came to reside in the parish, and even at this time, after a heavy continued fall of rain, and a rapid thaw of snow, is covered with water for a considerable distance on the eastern end: but within these eight or ten years it has been thoroughly drained, and now bears in all parts, and produces luxuriant grass. There can be no doubt from the formation of the elevated ground on either side of the bog, and, also at the two ends, that the whole of this land would be under water when the battle was fought, and for years after. In many places it is more than two hundred yards in breadth, but near the centre there is a slight elevation extending southward, which would naturally divide the bog of water into two parts. At this place, in Mr. Rankin's young days, there was a small narrow rude bridge, which went by the name of 'Branx Brig,' and which was always pointed out by the old people as the bridge over which part of the English army crossed when marching to Flodden Field.

"Now fill this tract of low land with water, and you have a substantial reason for part of the army deviating to the left, and crossing the burn at Sandy Ford, and on no other supposition, can a reason be given, why they should have departed from their direct line of march, unless the low ground to the south-east of the Blue Bell was impassable from its vicinity to the bog, which would, from the constant flow of water, render it completely unfit for the transit of a large body of men and horse, hastening with all possible speed to take up their position on Windylaw, and about the village of Branxton.

    *   *   •   *   *   *   *

"Opposite the formidable array of England's force, stood the Scottish army on the ridge of Branxton, waiting the approach of Surrey's army to commence the dreadful onslaught. To the extreme left, on the sloping part of Branxton Hill, looking towards Wark Castle, Home Castle, and Coldstream, were drawn up the wild and undisciplined Highlanders and stout Borderers under Huntley and Lord Home : to the right of these, looking north, those troops under Crawford and Montrose: a little further east the chivalric king, with many of his nobles, and best and bravest blood of Scotland; on his right, on the gentle slope of the eastern end of Branxton Ridge, was the right wing, under Lennox and Argyle, and the reserve, under Bothwell, a little to the south-east of the king's troops. In this position stood the contending armies, opposite each other, before the battle began—one elevated considerably above his opponent, and commanding one of the most splendid views in the country, looking over the greater part of Berwickshire and Roxburghshire, and even extending beyond the hilly county of Selkirkshire. With this beautiful landscape before them to the far west and north-west, and the English army below them, preparing for the bloody fray that was on the eve of commencement, thousands of the brave men of Scotland, together with their beloved king, viewed for the last time the country that gave them birth, and which was shortly to weep and mourn over the death of so many of her hardy and heroic sons.

"The commanding position occupied by the Scotch army on the heights of Branxton, gave them great advantage over that of their enemy; and although King James is blamed for abandoning his camp on Flodden Hill, yet, he must be considered by all who walk over the ground, and think for themselves, as having displayed good generalship in making choice of such a position, especially when he knew that Surrey was marching his army from Barmoor Common, with the determined intention of cutting him off from Scotland, by forcing him to battle, or with the view of plundering his kingdom.

"That part of Surrey's army which crossed the bridge at Twizel, and which was composed of the greater number of his troops, together with the heavy artillery, would, we may suppose, march directly on the road leading to Cornhill, and then turn on the Wooler road, instead of crossing by New Heaton to make a junction with that part which had forded the Till at Heaton Mill. The distance from Twizel Bridge to Branxton Church, by Cornhill, would be little more than five miles, and the road would be firm and passable. Three hundred years ago, the land by New Heaton would in some places be a mere rushy, swampy morass, besides being in many parts rough and uneven. This would tend greatly to retard rather than facilitate the hurried march of eighteen or twenty thousand men, encumbered with baggage and ammunition. To make good this supposition, we must carry our thoughts back to Sept. 9th, 1513, and not plan the battle field, and the march of thirty thousand men, as having taken place a few years since. Indeed, it will require no very formidable stretch of research to find out what lands have been made dry, what bogs and swamps have been drained off, within the memory of this present generation.

"Allowing these reasons to be not only feasible but probable, I place the junction of the two divisions that crossed the Till, at Twizel, and Heaton, as having taken place at Branxton, for the pool of water covering the bog, through which the small stream of Pallinsburn now runs, would be passed by the division that had crossed the bridge at Twizel on the west end, much about the same time as the troops which had passed the Heaton Ford, would be tramping over Branx Brig and Sandy Ford on the east end. The troops passing the west end would march immediately over the rising ground at this place, and on the low ground by Branxton Buildings, and form their positions under their different commanders a little to the south of the village, which I believe in those days extended considerably to the east and west of the church. A cannon ball weighing 13½lbs, now in the possession of Watson Askew, Esq., Pallinsburn House, was found a few years since when draining the upper or west end of the bog. May not this shot have been fired, when the right division was marching in the direction of Branxton, immediately after leaving the Wooler Road? Another ball in the possession of John Collingwood, Esq., Cornhill House, was dug up since my residence in the parish, near to the spot where such a number of bones were found about forty years ago by Mr. Rankin, when draining that part of the land, close to the ground taken up by the right wing under Ed. Howard. Both these balls are lead. I have an iron ball in my possession picked up by a man ploughing below the hill, nearly opposite the church. I may also mention here, that when widening the path to the church door, about nine years ago, we came on a deposit of bones close to the surface. I counted several sculls within the space of a yard square heaped, one on another. I can give no reason for these bones being found in such a position, unless we consider them as the remains of some of the men who fell in the village, and about the church, when the battle was fought, hurriedly collected together and buried in a hole, dug for that purpose, that they might rest in consecrated ground. My churchyard is exceedingly dry.

"I apologize for this short digression, and shall now proceed with my narrative. When marching from Cornhill the van guard under Lord Thos. Howard, his brother, and Sir Mar. Constable, which I will now call the right division, would first come in view of the Scotch army on the heights of Branxton Hill, a little more then a mile from Cornhill, on the Coldstream and Wooler road: the left division or rear guard under the command of the Earl of Surrey, and Sir Edw. Stanley, which crossed at Heaton Ford, would be in full ken of the Scotch force a short time before passing 'Branx Brig' and Sandy Ford, which, as I have mentioned before, lies a little to the south-east of Crookham.

"What I want, is to assign good and solid grounds for the proposition I now advance. I am well aware that no mention is made of these circumstances by any historian; but, I am also convinced that no one possitively contradicts them. After the English army had passed the bridge at Twizel, and the ford at Heaton, we are left to draw our own conclusions of the route each division took on its march to Flodden, with the exception of that part of the army which crossed at Sandy Ford. Surrey, we know from history, was most anxious to meet the king in battle, and there is not the least doubt but that he dreaded, with trembling and suspicious fear, his retreat over the Tweed into Scotland. Would not these reasons shew sufficient cause for the van guard to have orders to march as close as possible to the banks of the

Tweed, especially as we know, that in those days, and for a long period afterwards, that there were two fords by Coldstream, one at the mouth of the Leet, mentioned in *Marmion*, and through which General Monk passed his army on his march to London, soon after Cromwell's death, the other a little below Lennel. He knew that King James occupied the ground on Flodden Hill on the 8th Sept., the day previous to the battle, but during his march from Barmoor, where he encamped for that night, he was quite uncertain whether the Scotch army might not have been in full retreat for Scotland across these fords. Had this been the case, he would by marching the right division this way, have had a good opportunity of cutting off the rear, if not the whole of the Scotch army, and instead of fighting the king on Flodden Field, he would have fought him at Cornhill, or somewhere near that neighbourhood. Only let us suppose that these were Surrey's thoughts, and we have a good reason for his crossing the ford at Heaton, viz., that he might, by a quick march, come in sight of the camp at Flodden, and ascertain whether the king was there or not. Had the latter been the case, he could have pursued him along the road to Coldstream, and joined the van guard without much loss of time, or had King James's army been retreating to Scotland, he might have been hemmed in between these two divisions, and a slaughter equal, if not greater, then that on Flodden Field, have taken place.

"In Pitscottie's account of the battle of Flodden, published in 1728, we have no mention made of Sandy Ford, or in what manner the two divisions marched after passing the Till. In Hall's account of the battle, published in 1548, Sandy Ford is certainly spoken of 'as a small brook about a man's step over,' but he does not mention the junction of the two armies as having taken place before coming on the field of battle. In one place, he says 'wherefore the said king causing his tents to be removed to another hill in great haste,' which must have meant Branxton Hill. The position which he took up on this hill, shews I think, that he was expecting those forces that had crossed the bridge at Twizel to march on Flodden by way of Cornhill, and to pass by the west end of Pallinsburn bog.

"In a note appended to Hall's account of the battle, it is mentioned:—'The English army, while on the march, formed two large bodies, the foreward and the rear, commanded by the Lord Admiral and his father. Each division had two wings, viz., the Lord Admiral, on the right Sir Edmund Howard, and on his left Sir Marmaduke Constable : the Earl of Surrey, on the right Lord Dacre, and on the left Sir Edward Stanley. The attack seems to have been led on in the same order; though after the Lord Admiral requested his father's aid, the rear advanced, and left the foreward under the Lord Admiral to the right. Lord Dacre, however, kept his situation, which during the march was immediately behind Sir Ed. Howard ; whence he and, under his orders, Bastard Heron, were enabled to relieve Sir Edmund when discomfitted by Home. We are not so clear where Sir Marmaduke Constable fought, and whether his corps was joined to that of the admiral, or of Sir Edward Stanley. The former is more probable ; though as his body formed, during the march, as it were the van of Sir Edward, the latter supposition is by no means impossible. It was principally the difference between the order of marching, and that of the battle, which has confused the historians so much.'

"Now from this note, but more in particular from the nature and condition of the ground at the time of the battle, I assume that the two divisions, under their respective commanders, after passing the Till, kept entirely separate till they had formed in position to the south of the village of Branxton. King James had been warned of Surrey's having passed the bridge at Twizel, and he hastened to occupy the ridge of Branxton Hill, in the full expectation, we may presume, of seeing the English advance on him by that route, which would cut him off from his own country.[18] The

---

[18] Sir Walter Scott, in his *Marmion*, when describing the pass of the English army over the bridge at Twizel, seems to be of this opinion, for he could scarcely use the words he does, if the foreward had marched by Heaton, instead of the banks of the Tweed. In the former case, the king would have been between Surrey and Scotland, for Branxton Hill is considerably nearer the Tweed than Sandy Ford, and the king, had he wished to escape, might have done so without much peril.

"And why stands Scotland idly now,
Dark Flodden! on thy airy brow,

THE BATTLE OF FLODDEN.

39

different accounts are most perplexing and contradictory in many of their details, and it requires us to carry back our thoughts to the olden days of the beginning of the sixteenth century, and to judge for ourselves through what part of the country the different divisions marched after crossing the Till.

"Believe me, to remain, yours very sincerely,

R. JONES.

"To MR. ROBERT WHITE, &c."

Mr. Jones adds the following in a note, dated 16th November, 1858:—

"I have, since receiving your last letter, with the very kind remarks you have made, inquired more particularly respecting the Sandy Ford near Crookham. This ford is across the Till, and is considered, even at this day, quite good. Here it is where the boys bathe; the bottom is sand and gravel, the water is only about three feet deep, and not even this in summer. A little to the north of Etal Castle is *Watch-law*, said to be the place where Surrey's army encamped for the night; no doubt it has taken its name from that circumstance, as it is close to Barmoor Common. May not part of the army have crossed at this ford, which still retains the name, and the small burn, 'over which a man could step,' mentioned in history, be fabulous, unless the small stream of Pallinsburn, at its junction with the Till at this place, went by the same name. The cottages built here are called the Sandy Ford Cottages. This supposition would strengthen if not verify the Sandy Ford mentioned by Hall in his account of the battle."

With all deference to the opinions of Mr. Jones, the writer cannot assent to his view, wherein he supposes the foreward of the English army, under the Admiral, after crossing Twysel bridge, would advance forward on the road leading to Cornhill. It is more likely that the van proceeded up the western bank of the Till towards Heton, till Lord Howard came within view of the rearward, and then, assisted by sure guides, he led his battalions on in the most direct way to Branxton hill. He would elude morasses or other obstacles as well as he could, and we may be certain there were difficulties to overcome, for he took full five hours in going over as many miles. His father, we may presume, was behind him, and within reach, whatever might occur, so that it is not improbable but a part of Stanley's division might advance on the road towards Crookham, and approach the field by that quarter. Moreover, we are told the English were constantly in view of the camp at Flodden, till the smoke from that place hid the armies from each other; and again, we may be assured, it was not till the Admiral and Surrey, his father, bent their course full upon Branxton hill, that King James resolved to quit his position and occupy the latter place.

*　　*　　*　　*　　*　　*　　*　　*　　*

The poem of *Marmion* has drawn many a pilgrim to Flodden, who was altogether uncertain of the place where the battle was fought, and

> Since England gains the pass the while,
> And struggles through the deep defile?
> What checks the fiery soul of James?
> Why sits that champion of the dames
>   Inactive on his steed,
> And sees, between him and his land,
> *Between him and Tweed's southern strand*
> *His host Lord Surrey lead?"*

the writer has cause to believe that the actual locality was unknown
even to Sir Walter Scott himself. Visitors, however, may seek in vain
for the Cross of Stone upon the hillock, and the inscribed Well of Sybil
Grey, so associated with the death of the chief personage in that romantic tale. Besides, when the armies met, the smoke from the deserted
camp had vanished, and, except that caused by the artillery, the air
was clear; neither was dust, however fierce the turmoil might be, likely
to arise on a wild moor soaked with rain. But a poet, in the legitimate
exercise of his power, makes perfect what is defective; and it was as
necessary to Scott's purpose that he presented a picture to his reader's
mind—a conflict amid "clouds of smoke and dust," with the west wind
breathing upon it, as to garnish the story with the Cross and Well.
The attempt, as may be supposed, was eminently successful, for the
author, inspired as he was, threw over the scene the effulgent and im-
perishable light of his genius. No such attraction can be presented
by the sober relater of truth; yet to many the preceding paper will not
be without its value. Recalling what he was told, when a child,
of the dreadful encounter, and warmed like others by the poet's vivid
description of it, the writer has carefully sifted conflicting accounts,
separating refuse from the pure grain, whereby he might ascertain with
some degree of accuracy the whole circumstances of the battle, and be
enabled with his readers to gaze upon the ground where it was fought,
and think of the brave endurance, the devoted fidelity, the stern determination, and the terrible energies which were once called forth on that
place of renown.

Errata.
Page 12, line 6, dele " on the evening before the battle."